P9-ELP-926

THE OFFICIAL
MOVIE
HANDBOOK

THE OFFICIAL
MOVIE
HANDBOOK

SCHOLASTIC INC.

No part of this publication may be reproduced, stored in a retrieval system, or transmitted in any form or by any means, electronic, mechanical, photocopying, recording, or otherwise, without written permission of the publisher.
For information regarding permission, write to Scholastic Inc.,
Attention: Permissions Department, 557 Broadway, New York, NY 10012.

ISBN 978-0-545-62462-6

LEGO, the LEGO logo, the Brick and Knob configurations and the Minifigure are trademarks of the LEGO Group. © 2014 The LEGO Group. Produced by Scholastic Inc. under license from the LEGO Group.
BATMAN: TM & © DC Comics. © Warner Bros. Entertainment Inc. (s14)
The LEGO Movie © The LEGO Group & Warner Bros. Entertainment Inc.
KRAZY, KRAZY GLUE and The HANGING MAN logo are registered trademarks of Toagosei Co., Ltd. Used here with permission.

Published by Scholastic Inc. SCHOLASTIC and associated logos are trademarks and/or registered trademarks of Scholastic Inc.

12 11 10 9 8 7 6 5 4 3 2 1   14 15 16 17 18 19/0

Written by Ace Landers
Based on the Screenplay by PHIL LORD & CHRISTOPHER MILLER
Based on the Story by DAN HAGEMAN & KEVIN HAGEMAN and PHIL LORD & CHRISTOPHER MILLER
Special thanks to Matthew James Ashton
Designed by Two Red Shoes Design Inc.
Cover and additional illustrations by Kenny Kiernan

Printed in the U.S.A.   40
First printing, January 2014

Table of Contents

Welcome to
BRICKSBURG

Hello, citizen! And thanks for joining us in the wonderful world of Bricksburg!

Each day in our beautiful city is the best day ever because all of our citizens are superhappy. Just turn the page to hear from Emmet, one of our best citizens, why everything is awesome.

HEY, THAT'S ME! COME ON, LET'S GO!

EMMET

Emmet

HI! I'M EMMET, JUST A HAPPY CONSTRUCTION WORKER LIVING IN THE BEST CITY EVER, BRICKSBURG! WOW, I JUST REALIZED I MADE IT INTO THIS BOOK ABOUT MY FAVORITE PLACE . . . THAT'S SO COOL!

SPEAKING OF BOOKS, HAVE YOU READ **HOW TO FIT IN, HAVE EVERYONE LIKE YOU, AND ALWAYS BE HAPPY?** I ALWAYS KEEP A COPY ON-HAND. IT TEACHES YOU STEP-BY-STEP HOW TO HAVE AN AWESOME DAY. HERE, I'LL SHOW YOU.

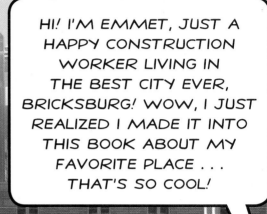

Octan

0-99
6981

STEP-BY-STEP INSTRUCTIONS!

HOW TO:

FIT IN!

HAVE EVERYONE LIKE YOU!

AND ALWAYS BE HAPPY!

 WARNING: Failure to follow instructions may result in a sad and unfulfilling life

HERE ARE MY FIVE FAVORITE STEPS FOR STARTING THE DAY.

STEP 1: **Breathe.**

It's easier than it looks. I can almost do it without thinking.

STEP 2: **Exercise.**

I am so pumped up!

STEP 3: **Shower and wear clothes.**

But not at the same time. I tried that once. It didn't go too well.

STEP 4: Enjoy popular songs, like "Everything is Awesome," and watch hit television shows, like *Where are My Pants?*

Ha ha—where ARE his pants? ⟶

STEP 5: And always obey President Business's instructions or you'll be put to sleep.

This guy is so cool! I always want to hear more of what he has to say.

SEE, IT'S SO EASY TO . . . WAIT, DID THAT LAST RULE SAY "PUT TO SLEEP"?!

OH, MAN, I LOVE THAT SONG! WHAT WAS I SAYING? EH, I DON'T CARE.

Me following the instructions. See how happy I was?

Then THIS weird thing got stuck on my back.

And now the police are chasing me. This is NOT cool!

I THOUGHT I WAS A GONER WHEN, SUDDENLY, THAT STRANGE GIRL SHOWED UP AGAIN AND SAVED ME.

THAT DOESN'T MATTER NOW. ALL THAT MATTERS IS THE THING ATTACHED TO YOUR BACK. IT'S THE **PIECE OF RESISTANCE** AND THE ONLY THING THAT CAN STOP PRESIDENT BUSINESS'S PLAN TO GLUE THE WORLD TOGETHER.

THERE'S A PROPHECY THAT SAYS ONE PERSON, **THE SPECIAL**, WILL FIND THE PIECE OF RESISTANCE AND SAVE THE WORLD. IT ALSO SAYS THAT HE OR SHE WILL BE THE MOST IMPORTANT AND EXTRAORDINARY PERSON IN THE UNIVERSE. THAT MUST BE YOU, RIGHT?

UHHH . . . YEAH. RIGHT . . . THAT MUST BE ME! ALL THOSE **AWESOME** THINGS THAT YOU JUST SAID!

I'M PART OF AN UNDERGROUND REBELLION CALLED THE **MASTER BUILDERS**. WE HAVE VOWED TO STOP LORD BUSINESS, OR PRESIDENT BUSINESS AS YOU KNOW HIM.

EVERY MASTER BUILDER CAN **"QUICKBUILD"** NEW OBJECTS OUT OF ORDINARY PIECES LYING AROUND WITHOUT FOLLOWING THE INSTRUCTIONS. JUST WATCH.

NEED A MOTORCYCLE? BAM!

NEED A MOTOR-PLANE? **BAM!**

WHOA, YOU SOUND COOL!

THANKS. NOW COME ON. WE NEED TO GO *SEE* VITRUVIUS. HE'LL TELL US HOW TO USE THE PIECE OF RESISTANCE TO SAVE THE WORLD.

THE PROPHECY

One day a talented lass or fellow,
a Special One with face of yellow,
will make the Piece of Resistance found
from its hiding refuge underground.
And with a noble army at the helm,
this Master Builder will thwart
the Kragle and save the realm,
and be the greatest, most interesting,
most important person of all times.
All this is true because it rhymes.

LORD BUSINESS

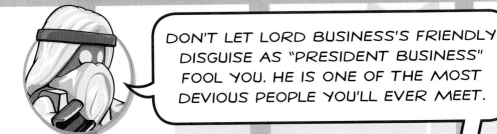

DON'T LET LORD BUSINESS'S FRIENDLY DISGUISE AS "PRESIDENT BUSINESS" FOOL YOU. HE IS ONE OF THE MOST DEVIOUS PEOPLE YOU'LL EVER MEET.

FOR YEARS I KEPT THE KRAGLE HIDDEN. BUT HE CAME AFTER IT, AND I WAS BLINDED IN THE BATTLE.

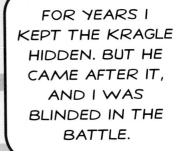

THAT'S RIGHT. I'M MISTER BIG BOY PANTS. AND THE KRAGLE IS MINE, OLD MAN. OH YEAH, THE KRAGLE. THE KRAGLE! **THE KRAGLE! HA HA HA HA!**

THE KRAGLE IS A WEAPON THAT SHOOTS LASER BEAMS OF GLUE. LORD BUSINESS WANTS EVERYTHING TO STAY HIS WAY, SO HE PLANS TO GLUE THE WORLD TOGETHER.

BUT IF THE KRAGLE IS CAPPED BY THE PIECE OF RESISTANCE, IT WILL LOSE ITS POWER. EMMET, YOU AND AN ARMY OF MASTER BUILDERS MUST STORM LORD BUSINESS'S TOWER TO STOP HIM AND SAVE THE WORLD.

PIECE OF RESISTANCE.

VERY SPECIAL.

SAVE THE WORLD.

PUT THING ON OTHER THING.

AND HERE I THOUGHT I WAS JUST NARRATING A BOOK ABOUT BRICKSBURG. THIS IS TURNING INTO A VERY WEIRD DAY. . . .

21

WE INTERRUPT THIS HANDBOOK WITH AN IMPORTANT MESSAGE FROM:

PRESIDENT BUSINESS

HEY, PAL! I'M PRESIDENT BUSINESS, THE OWNER, FOUNDER, AND PRESIDENT OF THE OCTAN CORPORATION . . . **AND THE WORLD**.

WE HERE AT OCTAN KNOW HOW HARD IT IS TO FIT IN AND HAVE EVERYONE LIKE YOU. SO, WE WANT TO SHARE OUR YEARS OF EXPERIENCE WITH YOU. IT'S A SIMPLE RECIPE FOR SUCCESS. JUST FOLLOW THE INSTRUCTIONS. MY INSTRUCTIONS.

HELLO, EXTRA ACTOR IN THIS SCENE WITH ME. HOW IS YOUR NORMAL FAMILY DOING?

WAIT, I CAN'T SAY THAT. WHO WROTE THIS MALARKY? **WHO?** WELL, FIRE THEM NOW!

TECHNICAL DIFFICULTIES

PLEASE STAND BY

HEY, BRICKSBURG, SORRY ABOUT THAT. YOU MAY BE ASKING, "PRESIDENT BUSINESS, HOW CAN I BE A BETTER CITIZEN AND EARN YOUR LOVE?" AND I WOULD SAY, "GREAT QUESTION!"

OCTAN HAS CREATED MANY PRODUCTS TO HELP YOU IN YOUR QUEST FOR NORMALCY. THINGS LIKE INSTRUCTIONS, GUIDELINES, AND STEP-BY-STEP DIRECTIONS TO LIVE YOUR LIFE.

AS WE LIKE TO SAY, "LET US DO THE THINKING FOR YOU!"

AND DON'T FORGET, FREE TACOS ON TACO TUESDAY!

WHAT CAN I SAY? OVERLORDING IS MY BUSINESS AND BUSINESS IS GOOD. BUT SINCE THE WORLD IS COMING TO AN EN — I MEAN, SINCE IT'S ALMOST TACO TUESDAY, I SUPPOSE I CAN SHARE SOME OF MY TRADE SECRETS WITH YOU.

How to Conquer the Universe While Making Everyone Love You

Step 1:
Breathe. Yeah, I guess that's an important one.

Step 2:
Amass a great deal of power by any means necessary. Like offering free tacos!

Step 3:
Impose rules. Lots and lots of rules.

BECAUSE I SAID SO!

I WANT YOU . . . TO FOLLOW THE INSTRUCTIONS!

BAD COP

OF COURSE, I CAN'T DO ALL THIS OVERLORDING ON MY OWN. MEET BAD COP, MY HENCHIEST OF HENCHMEN. WE'VE DONE SOME GREAT WORK OVER THE YEARS TOGETHER.

POLICED TO MEET YOU. ANYONE WHO GETS IN MY WAY IS GOING DOWN. LITERALLY. AND METAPHORICALLY.

ALTHOUGH, BAD COP DID LET THAT CONSTRUCTION WORKER GET AWAY WITH THE PIECE OF RESISTANCE. THE ONE THING THAT CAN RUIN MY PLANS. THAT'S SUPER-FRUSTRATING.

BUT HEY, NOBODY'S PERFECT. SO WHY DON'T YOU GO WITH BAD COP, FIND THE PIECE OF RESISTANCE, AND BRING IT BACK TO ME BY ANY MEANS NECESSARY.

DO IT NOW!

BATMAN

FIRST, WE HAVE BATMAN. HE'S AN INCREDIBLE, SUPER-DREAMY SUPERHERO. OH, AND HE'S ALSO MY BOYFRIEND.

I'M BATMAN.

BATMAN'S YOUR BOYFRIEND?!

unikitty

THEN WE HAVE UNIKITTY, THE MOST BUBBLY UNICORN-KITTY HYBRID YOU'LL EVER MEET. SHE LIVES IN CLOUD CUCKOO LAND: A CRAZY, COLORFUL WONDERLAND WITH NO RULES WHATSOEVER.

ANY IDEA IS A GOOD IDEA, EXCEPT THE NOT HAPPY ONES!

Hieeeee!

Hiii! I am Princess UniKitty, and I welcome you all to my Mega-Dreamy Dream Journal for my bestest friends in the whole wide world!

I know just the way to stop Lord Business from spreading unhappy thoughts. He just needs to see how much fun the happy thoughts are! **For example:**

What are your fave colors? Mine change every day, but right now I totally **love** mountain cherry, extreme watermelon, and sour apple.

And always remember, any idea is a good idea. Except the **not happy** ones.

BUT SOMETIMES, WHEN I THINK ABOUT LORD BUSINESS'S PLAN, I JUST GET SO . . . UH-OH . . . I FEEL SOMETHING INSIDE. IT'S LIKE THE OPPOSITE OF HAPPINESS. I MUST . . . STAY POSITIVE . . . BUBBLE GUM . . . BUTTERFLIES . . .

BENNY

REMEMBER THE FIRST ASTRONAUTS THAT WENT INTO SPACE? WELL, THIS IS BENNY, A CLASSIC SPACEMAN FROM 1980-SOMETHING. HE'S A LITTLE OBSESSED WITH SPACESHIPS.

IF WE'RE GOING TO STOP LORD BUSINESS, WE NEED TO GET TO HIS TOWER. AND THAT MEANS WE NEED A . . . SPACESHIP!

CAPTAIN'S LOG

ARRGH. WE TRIED TO STORM LORD BUSINESS'S TOWER TODAY. WE USED EVERY PLAN WE COULD CONCEIVE. THE RESULT WAS A MASSACRE TOO TERRIBLE TO SPEAK OF. BUT HERE GOES . . .

WE ARRIVED AT THE FOOT OF THE TOWER ONLY TO FIND IT GUARDED BY A ROBOT ARMY. AND LASERS. SHARKS. OVERBEARING ASSISTANTS. AND STRANGE, DANGEROUS RELICS THAT ENTRAP, SNAP, AND ZAP.

I LOST ME CREW. I LOST ME BODY. ME ORGANS WERE STREWN HITHER AND YON. I HAD TO STOW ME ORGANS IN A SEA CHEST AND REPLACE EVERY PART OF ME ONCE STRAPPING PIRATE BODY WITH THIS USELESS HUNK OF GARBAGE YE SEE BEFORE YE. ARRR, IT MAKES ME FURIOUS!

HMM, I'M KIND OF ATTACHED TO MY BODY, SO I PROBABLY WOULDN'T LIKE LOSING IT. THOUGH IT MIGHT BE COOL TO HAVE A SHARK FOR AN ARM.

HELLO, FRIENDS. VITRUVIUS HERE. BEFORE YOU CAN JOIN EMMET AND WYLDSTYLE ON THEIR ADVENTURE, YOU SHOULD KNOW ABOUT THE DIFFERENT REALMS IN THE UNIVERSE.

BRICKSBURG IS BUT ONE SMALL CORNER OF THIS DOMAIN. THERE ARE MANY DIFFERENT WORLDS TO EXPLORE. LORD BUSINESS ERECTED WALLS BETWEEN THEM, BUT WE MASTER BUILDERS CREATED SECRET TUNNELS ALLOWING US TO PASS BETWEEN THE REALMS.

FOLLOW ME AND I WILL BE YOUR GUIDE. UMM, BUT FIRST, WILL YOU HELP ME FIND THE NEXT PAGE?

THE BUSTLING METROPOLIS OF BRICKSBURG IS A CITY BUILT ON INSTRUCTIONS. EVERYONE PARKS BETWEEN THE LINES, DROPS OFF THEIR DRY CLEANING BEFORE NOON, AND NEVER FORGETS TO SMILE. BUT THERE IS A SECRET UNDERLYING BRICKSBURG'S SEEMING "PERFECTION."

OCTAN CORPORATION

AS THE OWNER OF OCTAN CORPORATION, PRESIDENT BUSINESS ORDERS BEAUTIFUL BUILDINGS TO BE TORN DOWN AND REPLACED WITH IDENTICAL SKYSCRAPERS. HIS GOAL IS TO GLUE THE WORLD TOGETHER SO NOTHING EVER CHANGES . . . PERMANENTLY. BRICKSBURG IS JUST THE FIRST BUILDING BLOCK TO HIS PLAN FOR WORLD DOMINATION.

SO . . . EVERYTHING ISN'T AWESOME?

THE CONSTRUCTION SITE

THIS IS THE CONSTRUCTION SITE WHERE EMMET WORKS. AFTER A LONG DAY, THE CREW MEMBERS ALWAYS GO OUT TO EAT CHICKEN WINGS AND GET *CRAZY*. NORMALLY, EMMET WOULD JOIN THEM. BUT ON THAT ONE, FATEFUL AFTERNOON, THIS IS THE PLACE EMMET FOUND THE PIECE OF RESISTANCE AND HIS LIFE CHANGED FOREVER.

I'M NOT GONNA LIE. THAT WAS A VERY WEIRD DAY.

THE WILD WEST

THERE'S PLENTY OF TROUBLE BREWING IN THIS ONE-HORSE TOWN. LORD BUSINESS'S ROBOTS ARE ALWAYS ON WATCH, INCLUDING DEPUTRON, CALAMITY DRONE, WILEY FUSEBOT, AND SHERIFF NOT-A-ROBOT. YET, I CALL THE WILD WEST HOME. WHAT BETTER PLACE IS THERE TO HIDE OUT IF YOU'RE A BLIND WIZARD WHO CAN PLAY A MEAN PIANO TUNE?

THAT MAKES, LIKE, ZERO SENSE.

CLOUD CUCKOO LAND

THIS WACKY INSIDE-OUT, UPSIDE-DOWN REALM THRIVES ON PURE CREATIVITY. THIS IS WHERE WE MASTER BUILDERS GATHER TO FORM OUR PLAN TO DEFEAT LORD BUSINESS. HOWEVER, THE PROPHECY DIDN'T PLAY OUT EXACTLY AS WE THOUGHT.

And now, a sneak peek at the new LEGO® Movie!

One average morning in the
city of Bricksburg, Emmet, the
most regular guy in the world,
woke up the same way he
did every day. He followed his
book of instructions on how
to fit in and ran through his
normal morning routine.

He greeted the day, smiled,
did jumping jacks, ate
breakfast, and watched
popular television shows on
TV. Then he went to work.

But wha[t]
didn't k[now was]
that too[k the]
beginni[ng of the]
most un[believable]
adventu[re of his]
entire li[fe.]

Emmet worked for a construction company that demolished every weird, creative building in Bricksburg. They replaced them with identical skyscrapers that always followed the instructions. No one knew why the buildings had to look the same. But those were the rules. And everyone knew that the best way to be happy was to follow the rules.

After work, Emmet had planned to join his co-workers for a night of delicious chicken wings. But just as he was leaving, a gust of wind blew his instructions out of his hand. He couldn't let them get away! He chased them down when, suddenly, Emmet saw a mysterious girl who wasn't supposed to be at the construction site digging through the rubble.

When Emmet tried to follow the girl, the rubble below him cracked open and he fell down into a huge hole! He bonked and tumbled until he finally landed at the very bottom.

When he looked up, he couldn't understand what he was seeing. Sitting in front of him was a strange-looking object glowing bright red. It was like nothing he had ever seen in Bricksburg. It was like nothing he had ever seen in his life. Emmet couldn't help himself. He touched it.

Instantly, a glaring white light flashed and Emmet passed out.

When he woke up, Emmet had no idea where he was. He was strapped to a chair in a strange place, and a very angry police officer was glaring at him from across the table. This was Bad Cop — the meanest, most ruthless officer in all of Bricksburg.

And he had one big question for Emmet:
"How did you find the Piece of Resistance?!"

#THELEGOMOVIE   WWW.THELEGOMOVIE.COM